Rush

Of

Many

Waters

Also by Pauly Hart

Novels:
By the Gates of the Garden of Eden
Novellas:
Superior Respondent
Ouesso to Epena
The Book of Lesser Voices
Mountain to Mountain
The Word of Yahweh unto Enoch
Empire of the Dragon
Finance:
The Richest Man In Babylon Continued Stories
Collections:
Sometimes I Write Tiny Stories
Adelphoi
Poetry:
Stupid Mind Tricks
Book of Love and Laughter
The Cross and the Poet
What is Poep?
I Love You More Than a Fox Loves Blueberries
The Night Clerk Held a Broken Pencil
Spontaneous Psalms
Kick the Prick
Exegesis with Co-Authors:
My Flat Earth
Biblical Cosmology, 8+ languages
Translations:
The Testament of Job in Modern English
Children's:
Mathmagician and Other Tales of Awesomeness
Periodicals:
Modern Epistle (1-8)
Microzine (1-5)
Rush of Many Waters (1-20)
With children authors:
Farrell Family Fables
With Co-Author Jennifer Hart:
Adulting: A Daily Guide on Being an Adultier Adult
Audiobooks:
Biblical Cosmology
Superior Respondent

Rush of Many Waters:

Volume Fourteen

By Pauly Hart

Contents

For Mafeking And Queen

A One Scene Play
July the Second, 2013
Written for JB Farrell, on his birthday

Historical Note: This is a fictitious account of a conversation had between Robert Badden-Powell and his superior officer Field Marshal Garnet Wolseley, before the infamous 217 day Siege of Mafeking, in the Second Boer War.

Historically, the defence of the town against the siege used all of the ingenuity that the young Colonel could afford, leading to a decisive victory over the Boers and of the elevation of Robert Badden-Powell to a British national hero. Powell went on to start the Scouting movement, for young men, namely in the Boy Scouts.

Actors:

Field Marshal Garnet Wolseley - played by Sean Connery
Colonel Robert Baden-Powell - played by Russell Crowe
"Jules" - played by Raymond Joseph Teller

Setup:

Wooden office, partially decorated with war memorabilia and fencing gear window overlooks lush countryside. A desk with papers and maps is stage right. A small stand with a carafe and two stemware is on the opposite side of the stage.

Period:

It is late afternoon to sunset, September, 1899.

(Curtain)

(Lord Wolseley sitting in chair behind desk)

(Powell enters in, stage left)

(Powell snaps salute)

Wolseley: At ease, Lieutenant!

Powell: Colonel, sir!

Wolseley: What what?

Powell: It's Colonel now, sir. I've got my promotion.

Wolseley: Oh jolly good man. Come sit!

Powell: Thank you, sir.

Wolseley: Eh, have some tea with me?

Powell: Beg pardon, sir?

Wolseley: I say old man, spot of tea or what?

Powell: Oh yes, sir. I'd like that very much sir.

Wolseley: Right. Jules! Tea!

      (Jules brings in tea, placing it too close to Wolseley, who grimaces and becomes annoyed.)

Wolseley: Oh bloody hell, Jules. I'll serve it. Be on your way man!

      (Jules smiles and nod/bows to both)

Wolseley: One lump or two, eh Colonel?

Powell: None, sir. Just like it the Queen intended.

Wolseley: Ah right, right! Long live the Queen!

Powell: Long live the Queen!

Wolseley: Ah so, now old chap, what do you make of the Afrikaners today eh?

(Wolseley hands Powell tea)

Powell: Oh I'd say that another war is eminent, sir.

Wolseley: Right.

Powell: I do believe that I'm quite sick of them sir.

Wolseley: Right.

Powell: And frankly sir, I do believe that I'd like to kick them in the teeth sir.

Wolseley: Ahem... Well well. Lets not be hasty then Colonel. Plenty of time for that sooner than you think my good man. Plenty of time... Now... Let me ask you this... Ever heard of Mafeking?

(Wolseley is ruffled, stands and looks off stage as you would look out a window)

Powell: Up north sir? On the border?

Wolseley: The same.

Powell: Well that's Afrikaner territory isn't it?

(Wolseley sits and fidgets for a while then regains composure)

Wolseley: Well. Not just yet I don't think. Look. It's ours if we want it at this point. The boys back home won't give us the go ahead to do anything yet. But it's on the horizon I feel it. Yes. We need that town, Colonel. It is vital to the Crown! We must have it and I want you to get it for us before the first gunshot is fired in this war that I know will be upon us tomorrow!

(Powell stands and almost drops tea)

Powell: Tomorrow!

Wolseley: Oh pish posh! Not tomorrow. I'm talking figuratively man. Sit, sit, I say and bring yourself together.

(Powell breathes sigh of relief, sits and straightens jacket)

Wolseley: Now. We need that town Colonel but we have to obey orders from home, yes? I just need you to figure out how to do it.

Powell: me sir?

Wolseley: you.

(Powell pauses and thinks, playing with his moustache)

Powell: Well... No... I could... No. Hmmm...

(Wolseley shifts uncomfortably)

Powell: Is there a roundhouse there?

(Wolseley frowns and consults maps on desktop)

Wolseley: No, just a thruway and a mechanic station.

Powell: But it's certainly no whistle-stop.

Wolseley: Certainly.

(Powell sits lost in thought)

Powell: May I see the map sir?

Wolseley: Oh just! Here!

(Powell stands and comes to the side of Wolseley's desk. Wolseley points on map)

Wolseley: Main roads are here and here. And we have our patrol shacks here and here and I think... Here.

Powell: Not really a commanding position.

Wolseley: But we make do with what we are given, what what?

Powell: Quite.

(Both are silent for a very long time, then Wolseley shouts and Powell jumps visibly)

Wolseley: Jules! Bring me my pipe!

(Powell picks up map and walks it over to window. Jules enters with pipe and fumbles about with stuffing it and lighting it, humorously)

Wolseley: Dammit man! Just give it to me.

(Jules fumbles about some more and almost spills the tobacco on Wolseley)

Wolseley: Out with you!

(Jules leaves, almost tripping on the rug. Wolseley stuffs and lights his pipe. Powell brings back over the map to the desk and places several different types of markers on it. Wolseley is interested)

Powell: Aha! There it is!

Wolseley: What? My ashtray?

Powell: No sir? Ah!

(Powell looks for ashtray, finds it and delivers it)

Wolseley: Thank you. Now, there *what* is?

Powell: My plan sir.

Wolseley: Explain.

Powell: right sir. I must presume that the Field Marshall is going to be declaring war *very soon* and so I must make my assumptions thusly. I cannot hold this town or take this town as it is...

(Wolseley starts to object but Powell's hand comes up. Wolseley sits back as Powell explains and puffs away dramatically on his pipe with great volumes of smoke. Powell points to various things on the map with great gestures)

Powell: If I may sir... *"As it is."* But I may hold it if I am inside and able to control it. The main road in from the north can easily be barricaded. From the inside the main problem is the east-west road. Unless I have a regiment, I cannot see any other way to do it unless I go in with a few men and recruit from within. Another Jameson raid will not happen here. We have not the numbers and we are not at war yet.

Wolseley: Yet.

(Powell begins pacing and using even larger gestures to and from the map while he moves pieces on map)

Powell: Quite. And so we must do to them what the Yankees did to us a six score years ago. Attack without attacking under the expectations of the enemy. What I propose sir is that I arrive to town under leisurely circumstances... by train. I then have following me, several men, acting under false pretenses as those would on holiday, to the town, and meet me there. My main goal would be to do a "check up and survey" of all of our supplies there.

Wolseley: You would have to ask the townspeople about that. They aren't too friendly to us now.

Powell: yes. But we already have three men there.

Wolseley: One man. A local.

Powell: Alright. We have one man in the town.

Wolseley: yes. Oh I see. Ha ha! we *already* have a man there. Jolly good. We need not get a foot in the door as we have already left our shoes there!

Powell: Well. Man. But we could inspect him. Inspect the shacks. Get permission to "guard" the shacks... Yes. We could do that. And then when they say "yes" to us. We walk in with a hundred men! and when I say walk in with a hundred, there will already be twenty of "us" there posing as vacationers, just change the clothes on the man. The man remains the same. Where there was one man, there will now be five score!

> (Wolseley jumps up from desk and begins pacing as well. Both men are very animated)

Wolseley: Aha! Doing our duty to the Queen whilst appearing otherwise!

Powell: We never fail when we try to do our duty, we always fail when we neglect to do it.

Wolseley: Well put! But how will you convince the people that they are not being over-run or besieged at that point?

Powell: Simply by telling them that.

Wolseley: Lying?

(Both men consult the map again)

Powell: not so lying sir. Just overstating the truth. We are "guarding our supplies". It just so happens that we need a great plethora of people to guard the supplies. And if we need to guard the supplies then we need to guard the surrounding buildings to the supplies. And if that, then the town that includes those buildings. So, in effect, we are guarding our supplies by occupying the town! Brilliant!

Wolseley: Brilliant!

> (Hearty pats on the back from both and a good deal of self congratulations then both sit and go back into thinking. Wolseley is casual about his pipe and bides his time while pouring drinks)

Powell: Now... After some time, as it is the custom with occupying forces, the local... People... The ah... Um...

Wolseley: 'Barolong Boo Ratshidi...'

Powell: Yes. But we can just call them 'Blacks?'

Wolseley: Calling them Barlong I would wager would do the trick, what?

Powell: Right. The Barlong will want to either help or rebel. They will choose sides quickly. So we must come with money or supplies ourselves... Surely since it's still an old mercenary town, there are bullets enough? Well. Aha. On second thought.. The men when they come in... In their luggage will be *"Survey Equipment"* or *"Safari Equipment"* and the like but it will really be in the likeness of war materials. Radios, rifles! ... And our jackets lined with bullets.

Wolseley: There's never enough bullets for the Dutch.

Powell: And we do pray that the Germanics and our own people of Britain will one day see peace with each other, I do not think that today is that day. Or tomorrow, as you say.

Wolseley: Quite.

Powell: So. We will buy the town instantly. We will throw a party and invite the entirety of them to join our cause.

Wolseley: Because by defending these three shacks of yours, they defend their own town.

Powell: Precisely. We will enlist the strongest and then enlist the next strongest. We will let them build their own army.

Wolseley: An army of Blacks?

Powell: I thought you said to call them Barlong.

Wolseley: All the same. I don't think that the Afrikaans will like that at all. I don't think the Queen will like it either.

Powell: Well, there is no other way. The people must be made free to fight. We all share the same color blood of this common goal.

Wolseley: So you have some men with you. Recruit the Barlongs, what about the English already there?

(Powell is back to thinking and stands to resume pacing)

Powell: They require no prodding I would wager. As a matter of fact they can be an equal squad of their own. Give the whites the buildings and give the blacks the perimeter. *"The Black Watch"*. They know the land better anyway. It was theirs to begin with.

Wolseley: Yes, but we traded fairly with them for that town. Everyone gets along there.

Powell: All the more reason.

Wolseley: What about defence? You can't just build walls or dig moats in those hills. It's naught but dust.

Powell: We have long-range sharpshooters. We won't let them near us. Ah. Wait. But a hoard would easily get by that. Barbed wire. Or not barbed wire at all. Hmmm.

Wolseley: Speak plainly man.

(Powell sits in the chair, lunges at the map, sits in the chair again and is silent for several moments. A smile spreads across his face and he comes around the desk to show Wolseley the map from his side. This makes Wolseley very uncomfortable)

Powell: Well it's been my experience that I cannot see barbed wire from a distance.

Wolseley: *Hmm.* Yes? Well, what of it.

Powell: Neither can anyone else.

Wolseley: What?

Powell: No one can. Not unless the gods of invention have created a better spyglass to outwit the mirage.

Wolseley: What are you...

(Powell moves pieces around on the map again)

Powell: No wire! Just the posts for the wire! And then *act* like there is wire there by ducking underneath when you come between the posts! Ha! It's brilliant! See... I build a perimeter around the entire town. That's only several hundred posts or road ties or *anything* I can find that will act as a fencepost... And then I do nothing with them. We will have men mimic the wire being there, and from a distance, say, just out of shooting range, they will think that we have circled the entire town about with wire! Under a barrage of sniper fire, no infantry unit wants to assault that!

Wolseley: Aha man! That's wonderful!

Powell: Yes! Yes! Wait. What's this?

Wolseley: That's TNT. We have about twenty kilos of it. half a crates worth.

Powell: That should be enough to be effective.

Wolseley: Against two armored units? What if there's twenty? Or more?

Powell: It's unavoidable. I wouldn't have enough anyway, even if we loaded down an entire boxcar full with it. I need another ruse. Except I will use all of my TNT to build it.

Wolseley: Build a ruse?

Powell: With shipping boxes.

Wolseley: Shipping boxes? No one's afraid of a shipping box!

Powell: they are if you paint it brightly and put "T.N.T." on the outside...

> (Wolseley sits and lights his pipe thinking)

Powell: I only need one, maybe two working models. I have one of the buildings sealed off, build a hundred boxes. Paint them all with "T.N.T." on the outside and fill them all with bricks. Except two.

Wolseley: Then... Then! *Great Scot!* Then you take those two and say: "Curse you Dutch dogs! I've got a hundred of these!" And you blow one up just to prove your point!

Powell: Yes!

> (Wolseley is impressed and stands, arm on the shoulder of Powell, they walk to center stage)

Wolseley: Ah Colonel my boy... You're one sneaky devil.

Powell: I believe that I should say 'Thank you sir.'

Wolseley: I must admit that you've got me on the ruse of your defences. So... Now... What about the townspeople? Say you have some sympathizers? Some spies who leak out and tell the enemy?

Powell: I won't let them sir.

Wolseley: Eh? How do you propose to stop them? That is a small miracle with invisible wire mind you.

Powell: They will be too happy to leave sir.

Wolseley: How's that?

Powell: Appease them sir. The way the Romans did it sir. Games, sports, theatre. It will be paradise on the inside sir for the most foul and the most unhappy of them. I pick out the ringleaders of the movement against us and turn them into the organizers of the activities.

Wolseley: Giving them even more power to rebel?

Powell: False power sir. They would be umpires. Coaches. Playwrights. Rebellion would be replaced with self importance.

Wolseley: Right. Keep a button on that.

>   (Powell gestures at the map and paces a little. Pours a drink for
>   himself and downs it, all the while seemingly thinking out loud,
>   growing more and more animated)

Powell: And... I was thinking that we could have some of our own spies during this *'supposed or probably going to happen tomorrow'* war. Many of my own men could spy out the enemy camp dressed as women. We could operate at night this way as well. Dressed in all black clothing. Sort of a camouflage if you will. Why we could even use an abandon train car to snipe at them if they get too close. I would dare say, that if they are unwise enough to camp along the tracks themselves that we could simply push a rail car down to them while they were all asleep and invade that way. Ha! If the tracks are greased properly they would make no sound at all! All that would be heard would be the mewling groans of the enemy being trodden underfoot.

> (Wolseley grows more and more uncomfortable at this talk and is almost revolted)

Wolseley: Jolly good... Jolly good.

> (A long pause while both are thinking and then both snapped back to reality)

Powell: it's certainly worth a looking into sir.

> (Visibly relieved that Powell has ceased talking war tactics)

Wolseley: So! Good man! You'll do it?

Powell: Was there ever any doubt sir?

Wolseley: None.

Powell: Then count me in!

Wolseley: For Mafeking and the Queen!

Powell: For Mafeking and Queen!

Wolseley: ...And a better South Africa.

Powell: Much agreed to that sir.

> (A pause, Powell sits, Wolseley sits behind his desk and cleans his pipe)

Wolseley: I wonder what, in all of this, will happen with those troublesome Afrikaners? Pretentious lot that. Calling themselves after the entire continent. Just like those troublesome Yankees. "Americans" Haw haw. Such arrogance.

Powell: Indeed sir.

Wolseley: And I can't help but think that they may yet try to take you on Powell. With all your cunning and deception, you hang on the edge of the knife, as it were. So much riding on ruses and trickery. One wrong move my man, and you lose your position.

Powell: Indeed sir. Yet I must stake my life on it.

Wolseley: And it comes to me that you might not come home.

Powell: Indeed sir. But I do have plans sir. I am always prepared.

Wolseley: Indeed you are. Well.

Powell: Well.

(Both stand and shake hands)

Wolseley: I guess this is it then Colonel. You leave as soon as you gather your men and your supplies. Hopefully tonight, by tomorrow at the latest. This must be done with post haste! God speed and return victorious!

Powell: Sir!

(Powell snaps salute and Wolseley salutes back)

Wolseley: Don't let anything surprise you out there.

Powell: Don't worry sir! A good soldier is never taken by surprise! He knows exactly what to do when anything unexpected happens.

(Powell exits stage left, Wolseley sits and reminisces)

Wolseley: What a fine young man. A very fine young man indeed. The best scout I have.

(Wolseley has mislaid his pipe and is suddenly very alert)

Wolseley: Jules! Damn it man! Where's my pipe?

(Curtain)

Shorts

The Monks of Mayhem

"I always thought that the one thing to remember was the timing" Jeremiah said as he pushed in the digits for the countdown.

"Not really," Thomas said, "It's more than the timing that's important, the most important thing is that it makes a really loud noise when it goes off."

Jeremiah finished typing into the code and threw the thermite charge into the window.

"Well, we should find out here in about twenty seconds."

They pulled open the gate and proceeded to the street.

"Should we stick around?" Thomas said

"Sure" said Jeremiah, it should be around ten more seconds from n...

BOOOM! a peal of thunder struck them to the bones.

"Was that us?" Thomas yelled, looking back towards the church

"No, i think God's giving us some cover!"

BOOM! Again, except this time not from above, but from much closer. The thermite charge had reached zero and detonated.

Suddenly it was raining.

Three hours later Jeremiah and Thomas were sitting in the sedan several miles away still monitoring the police scanner.

Nestled back in the modified pilot's chair, Thomas took a last drag off of a cigarette and pitched the butt out of the window. The rain had worked its mysterious job and put out the butt right as Thomas was done with it, causing the last puff to die in Thomas's mouth.

"Damn things will kill you", Jeremiah said.

"Don't you think that's what God keeps saying? Why do you think that he always puts them out on me?"

Suddenly the scanner burst in.

"Unit 12, Unit 12, be advised, units 14 and 18 report they are relieving you of your position. Make your report on your remaining shift back at the station. Have a good night Adam."

Jeremiah clicked off the scanner.

"That's our cue. C'mon old buddy lets go snag ourselves a copper."

With a silent purr, the sedan moved off thru the rain into the early morning dawn.

They knew the route that officer Adam Pulaski took, and it would take them past a Quik-Stop convenience store. Chancing that they could pull their deed off in front of the early morning crowd, they pulled in next to the dumpster lane at the store and got out.

They walked inside and waited.

Four minutes later, before they had a chance to look suspicious in the over-sized store, officer Pulaski walked in.

"Morning." said the clerk

"Morning." said the officer as he headed to the restroom. Jeremiah followed, then Thomas.

Jeremiah went inside while Thomas waited outside the door.

"Does he know anything?" asked Thomas, one hundred and ten miles later.

"Not a thing..." Jeremiah said

"Will he remember anything?" Thomas asked

"Not a thing..."

The silent body of Officer Adam Pulaski lay quiet in their trunk.

Poems

Of Christ and other men

Jesu joy of man's desiring
Failure in a Buddhists retiring
Burn in us your mortal gladness
Mohammed is a sorry sadness
We enjoy your glorious splendor
They enjoy the blood and plunder
Warriors in a righteous battle
They take jihad up as their mantle
Heroism is your spotlight
Hinduism is their birthright
You fulfilled six hundred sayings
Bahai fills only corpses' decayings

Oh Yahweh you are true and holy
Just and precious is your word
You sent us Jesu as your promise
He sent us the Spirit as he said
Other men may rise and fall
But your word stands above all
Jesu joy of mans desiring
Fills our lives up with your love

Lafayette

I guess I'm stuck in Lafayette once again.
It seems like it has become a welcome friend.
I tried to leave here once with my closest friend.
But I'm stuck in Lafayette once again.

It was the first time that I met her.
She was blonde haired, freckled, tall..
Pronouncing truth just like an angel.
A Latte' dream flown in for fall.

I said: "Howdy, how ya doin?"
She said: "Fine there, How 'bout you?"
I said: "Great, I like your scar."
And she turned red from head to shoe.

Now we're northbound for St. Paul,
In the beat up Volkswagen.
'Till we broke down on the highway.
You can tell we're on the ball.

We called help, it wasn't coming.
Just our luck, it started raining.
Now the van is just a lifeboat,
And we're stuck in Lafayette.

I guess we're stuck in Lafayette once again.
It seems like pain has become our closest friend.
We tried to leave here once with nothing but a grin.
Getting stuck in Lafayette over again.

the flower and the child

come walking in and love
come walking in
    eyes and ears open to life
and universes collide in respite
with discretion and respite
sharp nosed talons of hatred
come walking in
    scent and laughter wither them
with discretion and flowers

laughter sees immediately
the eyes and ears open to life
and flowers and children are common
in your wonderful kind of love
you told me i'm kind...
    kind of what???
    kind of scared
the kind that listens to you
and sighs with lostness
lost in your flabbergasting hope
lost in the immense joy of your smile
forever gone when you call me...
    call me what???
    call me sexy

                                     "Fretful"

A house full
of empty rooms
with only you.
    As you breathe
    the listless breath.
        (can I see
        you in misery?)

A garden filled
with empty roses
with only you.
    Crying the tears
    of undue fretfulness.
    Clenching the brand
    of hard shamefulness.
        (You see me
        in your misery?)

A head stuffed

with empty dreams
without you.
> Badgering the house
> of achieving greatness
> Screaming at the
> walls of beautifulness.
>> (beautifulness?
>> beauty?)

yes...

come in, open, realize, dream, believe.

Procrastination

I need more love
Today I'll seek joy
Tomorrow joy

But now I find
that all life's sins
defeat joy

destroy laughter

I am left
Baked and bruised
A Chrysalis, crushed

Love and peace inside
but poured out onto souls
contain nothing

Sunrise on hope
A smile, a kiss

and tender-heartedness

Crushed and bruised
The writing soul sees nothing
except his decadence

Why if I try, do I find
pleasure in crap?
pleasure in shit?

mediator

i plead innocent
for my crimes.
but was sentenced
all the same.

mediator.

he stood in my place.
he took the blame.
and died for me.
strapped to a tree.

mediator.

Jesus Christ.
took my sin.
i'm born again.
mediator.

love came over

love came over for tea

and sat down with me
it came over for tea it did
and i did not expect it

love came over for tea
and all i had was water
but it did not mind
for it was love

and you know how love can be

Spontaneous Psalm #12

Well I know I don't have to die Lord
Cause you died already
You're the pure Lamb
The lamb of God

When my voice is raw
And my fingers are bloody
I know you did it
You did it for

And I praise you
For who you are
Yeah I wanna love you
For everything you've
Ever done for me

But still I'd travel a thousand miles
To be right next to you

Essays

roses, petals, eggs

wow, i've noticed that drinking is NOT the answer for me. i am NOT doing that again. it was a mistake to start drinking without you there. i was just sooo bored. i had a couple of girls want me to buy them drinks... lol. i must have looked hot or something, that's what a girl at work told me anyway. oh, i just wanted to look good for you though. honestly i was miffed about jessica being there, but it was cool. you love her, and she is cool people. and you know, when i finally left town, i was almost ok to drive, i had eaten and drank a lot of water, and had rested... do it made me mad when jb and sarah decided that jb was driving me home, because as i came into lafayette, i was fine.

you are right. we were pretty patient with eachother. and still are. i just laugh about all the stupid stuff nowadays. :) it is kinda childish for us to hold these grudges with one another. i know that you have a lot of trust issues with mr. pauly to settle in yourself yet, but i am (believe it or not) trusting you just a little. when you wrote that you were smiling thinking of what was going thru my head when you told me i would be wondering what you were doing that night and with whom... it scared me. like... "uh, oh THAT'S what she meant by not having things worked out of her system yet." but you told me on the phone that you were just renting a video and going home... i hate to admit those feelings, but yeah, i did breath a sigh of relief. o h i know, that should be a trivial issue, but it kinda spoke to me, ya know?

i don't think i am ready to move to florida. too many things are left. too many choices need to be made. we need closure in our life. i don't think that i am ready to walk away from you either. i like you too much as a person. you are too much like miss perfect for me to wash my hands of you. you know? and it's not that EITHER of us has our shit together, but hey, two imperfect people have just as much of a chance together as two other imperfects.

hey, i know that you care if i die, and i know that i didn't kill the mother with three children. they were strong and brave and sought shelter away from the terrible monster. smart. oh, we both have our capabilities of being dumb, but at least you are a good mother. i ain't no good father. unwise and unfit is how i would best describe that guy. thinking that they were 9,10, and 11 was just what i was doing. and that was wrong. i hope abigail forgives me. and i pray that samson will find the strength to one day as well.

 you know i really do mean this shit that i put down. not so i can impress someone. i am done impressing you. it isn't the hunt i am after, and it's not even YOU that i want. it is our love. our marraige. our sanity. us. listen and hear that i am being 100% honest when i say this: you scare me even now. yes, the yo-yo thing is tricky. yes, you need to figure out what you want, and yes, i may be just what you desire... but please be sure.

 i sang and sang every song on the radio just like you. laughing crying and screaming all the way. but i hadn't found the perfect song until "i am ready for love" -that poem i mailed you. I AM READY to love. but to be loved? oh hell, i don't know. reasoning inside myself, i believe that it's possible. but who can say for sure. all i know is that i would like to start over. it has been a good week... it has been a shitty week. all of the blackness has had to be brought to the surface and looked at once again. and do you know what i found? i found that you are my desire. man, i miss our talks. our walks together. our soul searches. our movie-time. our weird schedules. our notes. our sex. our singing. our finding the new 'romantic' spot. our talks on God. our church time. our giving stuff away together. our love for people. our soul-gazing. our union. i miss the 'us' that had no flaws. you noticed that i never said goodbye to any of that. you were right. perhaps i never did say goodbye to the unity we had. it never crossed my mind TO DO IT.

 but, If we could lock the past away...step back through the doorway...this ride has just begun... i want to ride this roller coaster with that woman. shitty or happy. good and bad. nobody does life more fun than her. and i am still emotionally in love with her. that's why it's harder for me. for you, man! you must have some deep DEEP reasons to want to believe in us again, because i can't see how you do it without emotion. where did i touch you so deeply? where did i grow in your heart for you to come back? why have you decided this way? what is it about paul bradley hart that reaches you... to want to grab for him again. it isn't a lot of things i know, but i am capable of SO MUCH MORE BEAUTY! i just want you to know that i want to prove myself to you again. i do care. i do love. i have much love to give. i feel so deeply for you and your well being... it hurts, but feels good at the same time. i guess that's how you'll know. when it hurts it feels good.

I care and do not want to stop. I stopped caring for her long, long after we were apart. she stopped caring for me. and now you havent stopped. the reason that my ex didnt divorce me sooner, was that nick took a paternity test for caedmon, and her lawyer advised her that if she didnt want me to fight for rights to that baby, that she have it inside our marriage. you know, it went thru my mind that I could. but honestly, I didnt want any part of his life. that was all micheles decision. but she never came back. she never had hope for us. it was over. OVER OVER OVER! lol. and we both knew it.

so what is it in me that drives people away? manipulation. plain and simple. I want to control. this desire to have everything "mine". ha. bull-caca. that feeling leaves with each passing day. but i am noticing when i do it. i see the 'oooh yucky' part in me coming out, and just pause and think... ok, now what? and then let it drift away. can I ask you something? have you noticed a difference? has there been a change? i want to know. even if you never come back, be honest with me in this. can i make it as a human on this planet?

find me and know me that's how you will know. ya know? get to know who i am again, and you'll be able to figure it out. 'cause something weird has changed in jb and me. ha. maybe it's all been me. i told him that he didn't know me anymore, and he was like: 'yeah, i know.' hmmm. i actually feel comfortable confronting him now, and i don't let him push me around. that's unique. yeah, i am liking myself now that i don't 'know everything' and don't 'control' people. i have a hard enough time controlling myself.

honey, it's hard to leave this alone. i care for you deeply. i want to get to know you again. fuck roses. i love you.

A Guy Named John

So I stayed in the Bible for good. Learned to love it and learned how to study it even more than I already had. I took that VHS tape to heart but also took it with a grain of salt. There were larger truths out there and I was going to find them. Within the first eleven chapters of Genesis alone were some crazy nuggets. Just lying there, waiting to be had. I read and listened to those passages over and over until I almost have them memorized to this day. From day one until Abraham I had a thousand questions. So I started going through them one by one. Who were the giants? Who was Nimrod? Where was the Garden of Eden? Who did Cain marry? Where was the Land of Nod?

Where was the Tower of Babel. Too many questions to list here but you get the idea.

On my return from the Virgin Islands I moved back in with John Conrad and his buddies. John was a professional musician and producer and was always fun to be around. In our spare time when we weren't playing Age of Empires we would sit around and make music. This was John's passion and he helped me record a couple of great tracks and our friendship strengthened. I mentioned to him that I thought the world might be flat but the conversation never gained traction. We did have a lot in common though, conversationally, on the New World Order and several other things, as I've mentioned, like 9/11. Having someone to talk to in person besides on message boards or Myspace.com was important to me and I grew by leaps and bounds in research.

Another thing that I was going through about this time was I was involved with a pretty intense drama troupe. We were producing a play that was an analogy of the plight of the sinner involved with street gangs and how the power of "The Father" would draw them back to him. It was pretty interesting and they were happy to talk to me about end time prophesy (not my strong suit) as well as other Bible topics. Angels: yes. Creation: yes. Flat earth: nope, nope, nope. I must be a lunatic. So it was good to bounce ideas off of really "out there" Christians, just to test the waters. So far, I had no takers. Even my really good buddies Josef Lado and Drew didn't want to go there. We were too busy running an art studio and investing in digital currencies.

Skimming the truth

The word of God says that the sum of His words are truth. I have often come across this thought in my daily ponderings. If the sum of His words are truth, then what are the chapters? What are the phrases or sentences? Is it a whole truth, Or can we take it piece by piece? Is there only a small bit inside of the word that is true and the rest builds up to that truth? Or perhaps only a piece is "separated" or "holy", and the rest... well. No. All of

His words are truth. They are all true and truthful. And the sum of (or the completeness of them) is indeed all truth.

For God, perfect is perfect. Right is right and wrong is wrong. But most importantly true is true. God is best described as holy and true. No other two words describe Him so well. Even the angels as are written about them in the book of Revelations know this. They stand around and say: "Holy, holy, holy". They don't say: "Wonderful, powerful, lovely". Tell me, where is holiness? Where is truth? Can they be bought at the local market? Can they be purchased at the local convenience store? No dear reader, truth is found nowhere else but in the arms of God.

Let us look a deeper than where it is found. Let us look at what it is. What is truth? Even as technology changes and our laws change, does the truth change? Is it a relative subject under the influences of change and culture? Is it based upon laws? Upon morals? Perhaps it is based upon our abilities as humans (or inabilities). What is truth? God is truth. God is immutable and He never changes.

It was mid afternoon and the flies droned lazily about the musty old school room. Mr. Richards had taken his usual posture leaning on the table and was discussing modern church theology. Although not asleep, the students' glazed eyes were indicative of the utter boredom of yet another impassioned lecture about confession and baptismal rites.

Questions within each of the students hearts arose, tried to surface out of their heads, but eventually drowned again within the monologue. The students bodies were prone, but minds were listless, apprehensive, and on the majority, fifteen years old. Although not one year out of seminary, Mr. Richards had attained the heart of a scholar of many years.

Although each of the students were required to take the class we were all from various backgrounds and therefore were not in total agreement with the teachers appraisals of modern Christianity. Time grew long and surprisingly he touched upon a subject that he wanted a response to. What was baptism about? Was it necessary for eternal security? Was it sprinkling? Immersion? Was it important?

After some discussion he declared that the church had all the answers to these types of questions. That church polity was and should be the instructor for this spiritual dilemma. Although fifteen years myself, I had been brought up to believe that no matter what the church said, the Bible was always the final say involving dispute… especially those of a spiritual nature. So I raised my hand.

All eyes were on me. I asked Mr. Richards if he actually knew what the word baptism meant. No response. I asked for a dictionary. No response. After an uncomfortable pause, I got up and proceeded to get a dictionary from the front desk. The verdict for my sincerity? I was sent to the principals office.

Now I do not share this story to speak ill of any parochial Institution of learning, to expose the shortsightedness of any professor or teacher, and I am not bragging on the audacious qualities of my pre-pubescent self. What I am doing is asking why we are more concerned with the opinions of our local church or denomination than we are of our Bible? Should we blindly trust the decisions made by others or try to find the truth of any matter? Should we seek for ultimate truth and drink it whole… or merely skim the surface of it?